Shadow Kitties Proudly Presents:

Shadow Kitties Day at the Beach

A Counting Book

Written and Illustrated by Sommer Rayn

Today is a sunshine-filled day
The Shadow Kitties are at the
beach, ready to play.

The Kitties have never been to the beach before; they are so excited and ready to explore.

The beach ball looks so colorful and fun. Can you tell how many?

It looks like just one.

Look at these shovels, so shiny
and blue. How many are there?

We think
there are
two.

What are these green, leafy strands near the sea? They are seaweed from the ocean and It looks like there are three.

The Kitties found some starfish on the shore. They wonder how many.

Can you count them? It looks like there are four.

Out in the ocean, the Dolphins jump and dive.

The Shadow Kitties try to count them.

What do you think? Are there five?

Flying around the beach, the seagulls perform tricks.

Can you guess how many?

The Kitties found six.

The Kitties can smell the fishermen's fish. They smell like heaven.

The fish are lined up on the dock.

Let's count them. Are there seven?

The Kitties found shells and lined them up straight. They are so pretty and colorful.

How many are there?

Could there be eight?

What's this? A fisherman's net made of twine.

How many wooden floats are attached?

The Kitties counted nine.

The Kitties are on the bus and can't wait to visit again. Can you count the Shadow Kitties? There should be 10.

SOMMER RAYN is a self-taught artist who discovered her passion for drawing and writing at a very young age. Her style could be described as joyful and whimsical.

She is a strong advocate for animal rights. Her love for cats is evident in most of her work. Sommer has made it her life's mission to utilize her art in ways that will benefit animal rescues around the world.

She has a passion for assisting children with learning disabilities and special needs. Each time a new book is published, she donates several copies to various schools across the United States.

Sommer's book series 'The Shadow Kitties' focuses on the joy and playfulness of cats. Each book is beautifully illustrated with her signature black Shadow Cats.   The 'Shadow Kitties Day at the Beach, a Counting Book' is her latest book in this series.

Sommer's book series 'My Enchanted Earth' focuses on stories that are filled with uplifting messages that reinforce life is full of joy, gratitude, positive self-worth and love. Some of the books in this series are: Sprinkles the Happy Cupcake, Rascal the Raindrop and Stormee the Umbrella.

'If I have made you smile or created happiness within you, that is the true measure of my success.'

~ Sommer Rayn

www.ingramcontent.com/pod-product-compliance
Lightning Source LLC
Chambersburg PA
CBHW041612120626
46551CB00002B/410